E&L 19 (08/02)

Renfrewshire
Council
DEPARTMENT OF EDUCATION
AND LEISURE SERVICES
LIBRARIES

Thank you for using _____
Library. Please return by the last date below.
Renewals may be requested in person or by telephone.

Bargarran 0141 812 2841	Bishopton 01505 862 136	
Bridge of Weir 01505 612 220	Central 0141 887 3672	
Elderslie 01505 322 055	Erskine 0141 812 5331	
Ferguslie Park 0141 887 6404	Foxbar 01505 812 353	
Gallowhill 0141 889 1195	Glenburn 0141 884 2874	
Johnstone 01505 329 726	Library HQ 0141 840 3003	
Linwood 01505 325 283	Lochwinnoch 01505 842 305	
Mobiles 0141 889 1195	Ralston 0141 882 1879	
Renfrew 0141 886 3433	Spateston 01505 704 527	
Todholm 0141 887 3012	Toy Library 0141 884 8000	

LEGENDS OF THE BORDERS

WENDY WOOD

Legends of the Borders

*Stories for the young
and the not so young*

IMPULSE BOOKS

ABERDEEN 1973

First published 1973 by
Impulse Publications Ltd.,
28 Guild Street, Aberdeen
SBN 901311 34 0

Printed by Gee and Son, Denbigh

Contents

Sir James The Bully

Because the evening sky was stormy behind the Border hills, the lone traveller was relieved to hear the sound of pipes, and, rounding a corner, was able to join the piper who was going home with his cow. The stranger soon made it clear that he would be glad of shelter for the night.

" Aweel, ye're welcome tae sic fare as mysel' and my wife can offer," said the piper, seeing by his companion's attire that there was no need to apologise for their humble home.

The evening was spent in piping and singing, and the stranger was not backward in providing his share of entertainment. He learned that the cottar's name was Bartram, that he was a cobbler, and had but one cow for lack of land.

The following morning the guest smiled when he wakened to hear the sound of larks and the lowing of the cow, and sat hungrily to his breakfast of porridge consumed with a horn spoon from a wooden coggie. It was natural for the host to enquire the name of his guest, and little did he expect the reply he got.

" My name is James," then there was a pause, " Stewart," and a longer pause, before, with a smile, he added " King of Scots."

At first the cobbler did not believe it, but when he suddenly realised the truth of the statement, he and his wife were on their knees.

" I have reason to be grateful for your hospitality," said James.

" Where do you go now, Sire? "

" I go home by Drumelzier." At this information Bartram insisted that he accompany his sovereign, and not without good reason, for the owner of Drumelzier Castle, Sir James Tweedie, was an arrogant bully who demanded tribute from all who passed by. Indeed in terms of the time by a nautical observer " he required of people that they strike sail, salute, and pay homage, and are like to return from wherever they came, not without some marks of disgrace." The King assured the cottar that there was no need for his company as he had arranged for his courtiers to be in the vicinity, and had a silver whistle with which he could summon them. But the cobbler was adamant and they set off together. Sure enough two retainers of Drumelzier leapt out on the two travellers.

" Doff your bonnets to Sir James Tweedie," they shouted. " How dare ye pass without paying respect? "

The cobbler was kicked to the ground, and King James was dealing with the other fellow threatening to flog him, but making small headway against clever singlestick work. Then the sound of the silver whistle shrilled above the din of the stramash and a few minutes later the mounted nobles had not only quelled the attack, but had introduced Sir James to his sovereign. The culprit knew that it would be of no use to plead that the King had been in disguise, for to have attacked the defenceless poor was an even greater crime in the eyes of James. To have assaulted the royal person most assuredly meant a sentence of death. Amazed and abashed, Sir James listened abjectly to the demand that he attend the Court at Holyrood next day. The same order, but in a kindlier tone, was given to the cobbler.

So the following day at Court, overcome by the grand surroundings, humble Bartram waited behind the pompous figure of Sir James Tweedie, but was called first to the royal presence. He faced the figure of his king who was resplendent in velvet and jewels, and compared him with the man in dusty peasant clothes who had eaten cheerily from a wooden coggie.

" This worthy man," the King explained, " gave shelter and food to one whom he thought to be as poor as himself. Moreover he defended me to his own personal risk and injury. I therefore grant to him an extension of his land to the amount that will enable him to keep a mare and foal, a brood of pigs and five soums (pasture) for sheep on Holms Common."

It was a dazed cobbler who returned home that night to share his joy.

Sir James Tweedie was rebuked before the Court and deprived of much of his land; from then onward the family did not prosper, which was also partly due to a vendetta with the Veiches which lasted into the next century.

The name Tweedie is said to be due to a nobleman of the district who had been away at the Crusades for a year. On his return he found his wife with a small son, whom she said had been fathered by a magic knight who had risen from the waters of the river Tweed. It is doubtful if the husband credited such a tale, but perhaps he realised that a year was a long time to have left a bonny young wife alone, and he accepted the boy and called him ' Tweedie '.

The ruins of Castle Drumelzier with its memories back to the fourteenth century are in the farm steading of Drumelzier Place Farm, and the remains of the three storied tower, built of varied local rough stone, is in contrast to the surrounding comfortable Border hills. In a vault under the small local church lies Sir James who died in 1612 and, outside it, is a replica of the family crest from the Castle with the family motto " Thole and Think ". His career would imply that he did not think very deeply, and that it was other people who were required to thole (tolerate).

Owing to debts the property passed to the Stewarts of Traquair in 1622.

The Tinker

It was an early day in June and the messenger to Newark Castle was afraid to face the Douglas because he bore ill news. Breathlessly, he announced that his master's betrothed, Lady Harriet of Thirlestane, had eloped with the Earl of Ross. Hot temper over less outrages than this was natural to the members of this clan, and with an oath, Lord Douglas mounted his swiftest horse, shouted to two attendants to follow, and sped through the gate like a flung spear. There he halted at the choice of roads. Which way had they gone? The King's road north by Peat Law, the Three Brethren, Broomie Law and Brown Knowe, the road that was well known to Edward I of England, which led to Traquair and Peebles? Or had they held west by St. Mary's Loch and Moffat? There were no travellers about except a Tinker on a stout pony.

" Have you seen anyone on the road? " barked the Douglas.

" Aye," replied the Tinker speaking irritatingly slowly, " I did see a knight on a black horse and a lady on a grey mare. They came through the north

gap at daybreak on the way to St. Mary's chapel where I doubt they'll be man and wife by noo."

" By Saint Ninian she shall be a widow before night falls," said the Douglas pressing spurs to his horse and not even noticing that the Tinker was following hard on his heels.

It was nine miles by the Yarrow Water before the sheen of the loch implied another mile to the little chapel sitting high on Henderland Hill. A scared priest came to the door at the sound of clattering hooves, for these were the unchancy times of religious division, but he had no time to ask questions before the Douglas flung himself from his horse and demanded of him, " The knight and the lady? Which way did they go? " The priest denied that any such people had passed.

" You're hiding them! " and the infuriated man clanked into the chapel to find only silence and candles that bowed to the draught of the open door.

" You married them! " he shouted at the priest.

" Sir, I am in holy orders and you should not accuse me of a lie."

Douglas turned to the Tinker.

" You scoundrel! You've deliberately sent me astray! "

The accused remained calm.

" Aye, I did so. They went by the north gap."

In fury the Douglas raised his sword and smote

the Tinker's face with the flat of the blade which brought blood — and action.

" You dare to strike what you believe to be a Tinker and an unarmed man? I will teach you better manners, Lord Douglas," and from under his tattered cloak the Tinker suddenly produced a sword and used it with such effect that his opponent was hard pressed. The distressed priest retired hastily into the chapel to pray. It was ten minutes of clash and grunt and stour before a cunning flick of the wrist sent the weapon flying out of the Douglas grip to lie on the ground, its owner disarmed and dismayed.

" Beaten by a Tinker! Me! A Douglas! I am for ever shamed. Who taught you such swordmanship? What is your name? "

" My name is Jock Johnstone." It was a common enough name on the Borders and the Douglas suggested with commendable forgiveness that such a good swordsman might join his service.

" I think, my lord, that you might learn something of my trade and with it swordsmanship at practice with me." Before his opponent could find words to avenge the insult, the two attendants rode up and, seeing their leader disarmed, rushed into the fray shouting " A Douglas! A Douglas! "

Great was their distress when, with one gesture, the Tinker had cut their horses' reins and had the

16

two men trussed on the ground before him. Even their master had to laugh at the expressions of their bewilderment.

The Tinker picked up the sword and handed it to the frustrated knight.

" Do not be distressed, my lord, for though I look like a Tinker and am a Johnstone, I am also Lord of Annandale." But the Douglas was not easily appeased.

" Why should you take upon yourself to interfere in my domestic affairs? "

" Because the Lord Ross is my friend and the Lady Harriet desired to wed him. Moreover, he is a better swordsman than either you or I, and murder by either of you would have brought out the clans and added many another good man's death, and," he added with a laugh, " it would not have brought so much as one extra beast to the byre! "

The Douglas began to find consolation in the position.

" Lady Harriet is the daughter of Sir Francis Scott of Thirlestane, and I do not think he will approve of her marrying a man who already has had three wives. There was Agnes, Margaret and Anne. Earl of Ross he may be, but he is an auld rip, and she'll find out that an auld man is just a bedfull of banes."

" Well, you'll need to thole what you cannae mend, and I'll add a wee word of advice, and that

17

is never strike a Tinker for he might be the Lord of Annandale."

The contract of marriage between Harriet of Thirlestane and the Earl of Ross is dated 16th June 1731. The lusty noble was well on in his seventies, and did not long survive his fourth matrimonial adventure.

Grizel

Sir John Cochrane, far from his home in Ochiltree, Ayrshire, stared gloomily at the grimy floor of his prison in the Tolbooth of Edinburgh. It did not seem long since he had been in Holland with Monmouth planning their landings and assault upon the Catholic person of King James VII. But Holland, though generally anti-Stewart, had glimpsed the possibility of her own William's Crown Matrimonial, and so had unexpectedly withdrawn support. This had caused Monmouth to hasten his plans, resulting in disaster for him after his landing in the south of England, and for Argyle in Scotland where his followers, Sir John Cochrane and his friend Hume of Polwarth, were both taken prisoner and were now under sentence of death. It was small comfort to Sir John to know that his father, Lord Dundonald, was using all his influence to try to save his son, because the prisoner knew all too well that the messenger of death was already on his way from London with the royal warrant for execution.

The family, including his favourite daughter Grizel, just turned eighteen, had already paid their

last sad visit to the Tolbooth, but they would not leave Edinburgh until after the tragic day that lay so near ahead.

Grizel could not rest; whatever she was doing she seemed to see that Courier speeding northward with the fatal bag. That was why, one morning early, she left their lodgings secretly, and took the coach on the south road into England as far as Belford in Northumberland. There she visited the home of her old nurse.

" Goodsaikes, darlin'! What be you adoing of here? " asked the astonished woman. Grizel explained the terrible circumstances and found it as easy as in her babyhood to get her own way and borrow the male attire of her nurse's absent son, and take the loan of one of his pistols.

As every hour mattered, she set off in the twilight on foot, for the Messenger would spend the night at Buckton Inn and she must get there first to avoid suspicion. On arrival she found a shadowed place in the deep inglenook, and sat getting more and more nervous as the night wore on and the room filled with country labourers. At last she heard the sound of a horse at the door, and she trembled with fear and excitement as the Courier entered, a big man, with the bag containing the fatal paper slung over his shoulder. He partook of a hearty supper with plenty of good ale, and then retired to his bed in a small backchamber which the importance of his office allowed him to claim.

The inn emptied. It was no unusual thing to have a beggar at the hearth for the night, so the innkeeper also went upstairs to bed. Soon there was no sound but the snoring of the Courier. Grizel crept to his room in the hope that she would be able to lift the bag and extract the wanted document, but her hopes sank when she saw it acting as a pillow under his head. The outlook appeared hopeless, but in the dim light she saw his pistol on the table by his bed, conveniently to his hand. Hardly breathing with apprehension, she lifted it, removed the charge and, setting it silently back, tiptoed from the room. A few seconds later she was out in the dark night, sometimes walking, sometimes running along the highway (now the old road from Dechant) till she found a spot just suited to her purpose at the first junction where the hill turns down to Fenwick. There, a stand of firs on a mound commanding the road, is still known as ' Grizel's Clump '. Crouching in the undergrowth, Grizel waited, trembling with apprehension, only the thought of her father's greater danger keeping her to her resolution. At the first silent silver streak of dawn, before the first bird lifted a voice, she heard the clatter of a galloping horse and saw the dim figure of the tall rider coming nearer and nearer. What if she missed? What if she killed him? Grizel did not care, he had death in that bag. She leapt out and pulled the trigger, and missed! But the surprised and frightened horse reared, throwing its rider heavily to the ground, where he lay as one dead. Grizel calmed the horse, and wrenching the bag from the unconscious rider, found a rock which enabled her to mount, and galloped away towards the north. When she felt that she was at a safe distance, she opened the bag, and searching frantically through the papers, at last found the Order of Execution signed by the King.

She tore it into tiny shreds that fluttered away in all directions on the wind and, mounting again, made her way more leisurely to the Capital with a light heart. At least the warrant had been delayed.

It was this delay which gave Sir John's supporters time for further action resulting in a reprieve. But not till he was free did he learn that he had to thank his courageous young daughter Grizel for saving his life.

The Tailor's Apprentice

The custom of tailors visiting outlying farms to work lasted well into the nineteenth century. They made up the home-woven tweeds into suits and skirts, or cut down the farmer's worn trousers to make breeks for a laddie, and brought with them not only their tools but all the clash of the countryside. So the farm of Deloraine should have been pleased to welcome the tailor. But the farmer's wife was a crabbit buddy and definitely the boss, and the tailor's nervousness was added to by the inexperience of his young helper, it being his first day at the trade. As they had walked up far from the banks of Ettrick Water they were each given porridge and a bowl of milk. The milk, being unusually thick and creamy, was finished before the porridge.

" Guid fare, wife! " said the tailor, " but a sup mair milk wad be welcome."

" Milk is short the day," she grumbled as she waddled to the dairy, jug in hand. Alec, the apprentice, full of curiosity, followed her without being seen or heard and was surprised to see that the dairy was devoid of the usual full basins and

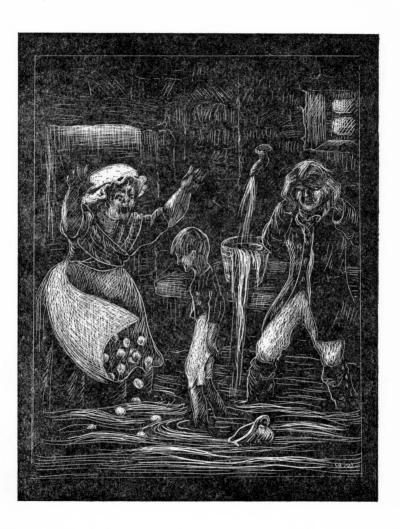

crocks, and that the farmer's wife turned on a spigot in the wall from which milk flowed freely. He was back in his seat before the jug was full and said nothing to his master. They settled to work while the wife went to the barn to collect eggs.

Alec was soon bored with the job of unpicking an old coat, and his eyes and ears were alert for any diversion. A pig grunted and he was immediately at the window.

" It's a grumphy! See! It's a grumphy! "

" Aye, I see it's a grumphy. Sit doon."

Soon after this a hen cackled.

" It's a hen! See! It's a hen! "

" I ken it's a hen. Sit tae your work ye gommeril."

There was a sound from a cupboard and Alec was up again.

" It's kittlins! See! Kittlins! "

" Aye, I see it's kittlins. You get your dowp under you and tae work." Silence and snipping prevailed for a while and then Alec was delighted when his master commented,

" There mun hae been ower muckle salt in yon parritch, I've an awful drouth. The old curmudgeon winna gie us ale, but I could dae with mair o' the milk."

Alec was off like a flash with the jug in his hand on the way to the dairy.

" I ken whaur to get it," he shouted back as he

26

turned on the spigot in the wall, and grinned as the milk flushed out. The jug being full, he turned off the spigot, but that made not one whit of difference, the milk still flowed plentifully. He grabbed a bucket, hastily turning the tap this way and that without result, for the milk still gushed out, over-filled the bucket, spilled over the shelf and splashed onto the floor. In a panic Alec called to his master.

"Ye wantit milk," he yelled. "Weel, ye've got it noo!"

"Ye young gowk! Turn it aff." But the tailor himself was no cleverer in his efforts, and young Alec was gleefully learning new swear words as the milk splashed everywhere and was soon up to their ankles. When the wife returned with her apron full of eggs to see the dairy awash with milk, she let go her apron and dropped all the eggs.

"Ye meddlesome fools!" she shrieked. "Ye've milked all the kye in the district o' Kershope frae the Insh to Buccleuch. The milking lassies will be sitting aneath the coos and not a drop will they get. Singing to them or no singing to them, not a drop will they get. You have ilka beast in the countryside dry," and she turned off the spigot.

The frightened tailor and his apprentice returned hastily to their work and skimped work it was in their desire to get out of the farm of Deloraine and away from one whom they now knew to be a witch.

27

" One word aboot this to anybody," she warned, her eyes glaring, " and I'll put a drouth on ye that the whole of St. Mary's Loch wadna satisfy."

Was this dame ahead in agricultural matters with a tank for milk concealed in the dairy wall, and was she deliberately conveying the suggestion of witch-craft to prevent imitation? Anyway, though the tailor and his young apprentice had many a tale to tell at the farms they visited, they never, until she was dead, related their experience, or hinted that the wife of the farm of Deloraine was a witch. Had they been tempted, one look at the size of St. Mary's Loch would have silenced them.

Whuppety Stoorie

The widow went to and fro, to and fro to the pig-
house with the bairn at her heels. Even during the
night she would rise to take a look at the grumphy.
The rent for the cottage was due to be paid, but
mercifully the sow was due to farrow. Martha was
a good mother who adored her son, but, in contrast,
a sow is a kittle parent, apt to tread on or overlay
her offspring, and so needs constant watching.

Martha's small son was bedded and she herself
ready to retire, but she took the lantern to have
one more look at the sow. The minute she set eyes
on the creature, she suspected that something was
desperately wrong. It lay with closed eyes, jerking
as if in a fit, foam and blood oozing from its
champing mouth. The nearest neighbour was five
miles away and something must be done quickly.
She poured a bucket of cold water over it and by
its lack of reaction she thought she had killed it.
It must have eaten something poisonous, Martha
thought, and in a panic of woe she burst into tears.
How would she find the rent? She had been expecting at least five or six piglets. With her apron to

her eyes, she did not see an old woman in an old-fashioned dress coming towards her.

" What gars ye greet? " the woman asked.

Martha pointed to the sow.

" Due to farrow, it's dying and the rent's due."

" Whisht, whisht," said the old woman, " it's like to die true enough, but I could save it, aye I could so."

Hope rose in the widow like the morning sun, she knew that these old women often had special cures for man and beast.

" Please," she stammered, " Please help, I'd give *anything* to see yon beast on its feet again."

" Bind yourself to that promise, and I'll dae it."

Martha willingly bound herself, seeing a way out of all her trouble. Just then the lamp blew out, but Martha could hear the old woman murmuring strange words over the sow which suddenly rose with a grunt, walked around, then lay down and proceeded to farrow. Ten piglets were soon at their breakfasts.

" How can I thank you? " Martha exclaimed. In her excitement she had forgotten the promise that she would ' give anything '.

" Now for your bargain," said her visitor, and the widow wondered what in her humble house she could part with.

" I'll tak' the bairn."

31

" Oh no no, you can't, not my wee laddie! I've got an old brooch I'll give you . . . "

" I'll tak' the bairn."

" I've a pair of fine linen sheets . . . "

" I'll tak' the bairn, and I'll be back in three days for him unless," she paused, " unless you can tell me what is my name," and she hirpled away down the path.

The mother went slowly into the house to take a look at her sleeping son. Guess the woman's name? How could she? Sleep was impossible and she sauntered into the wood behind the cottage. The moon was up and made confusion with the black shadows among the tree trunks, but Martha knew every stick and stone on the hillside, or so she thought, until she found herself looking at a dark slot that implied a cave. So hidden it was that she must have passed it many a time without seeing it. She did not dare to enter, she had had enough of strange ' ongauns ' for that night, but she heard the whirr of a spinning wheel and laughter and a voice that sang.

> *Little kens the good dame at hame*
> *That Whuppety Stoorie is my name.*

Martha fled back home repeating the name " Whippety Stoorie " continually, almost looking forward now to the old woman's next visit. In three days she came again. The laddie was playing with pebbles at the cottage door and crept to his mother's skirt at the sight. Martha saw no reason not to tease the cruel creature, so she began to beg her to call off the bargain, but the old wife would have none of it, she would take the bairn, and stretched out her skinny hand towards him.

" Just a minute," said the mother as the child started to cry, " you promised that if I could tell you your name you would not take him."

The old woman laughed.

" Your name," said Martha firmly, " is Whuppety Stoorie." The old woman was dumbfounded but could not deny it, and left in a furious temper.

" What a queerlike name! " remarked the laddie.

True enough! But it is interesting that the Scots dictionary gives upput (and the ' u ' is often like the Welsh pronounced as ' oo ') as ' the power of secrecy to prevent discovery ' which is just what the story is about, and is in keeping with general folklore belief in the power over a person when you can use their name.

Tamlane

The Ettrick Forest provided the finest hunting in the Borders, and young Tamlane was thrilled at the age of nine when his uncle let him join the hunting party. The horse was somewhat big for him, and after a few kills his enthusiasm was a little dulled, and the heat, combined with the murmurous rustle of the leaves, made him drowsy so that he lagged behind the main body of riders. As the horse slowed its pace, the young rider dozed, slept, and fell to the soft forest floor. From there the Faeries took him to live with them in the woods of Carterhaugh, where Yarrow and Ettrick waters meet, and he became faerie ' in lyth and limb '.

On the hill, one and a half miles away, Oakwood Tower still stands, tho' its oaks are now mixed with other trees. The tirling pin is worn thin on its door, and it is long since riding horses were tied to the ring beside it. From the little windows of its corner turrets, one of which shows the crescent crest of the Scotts, Janet, the daughter of the house, could look past the orchard (where apples still ripen) and walled garden, to the woods of Carterhaugh, which held the fascination of being forbidden territory.

I forbid ye maidens all
That wear gowd in your hair
To come or gae by Carterhaugh
For young Tamlane is there.

Apart from being a typical Border lass with a mind of her own, the beauty of the woods would be enough to tempt Janet in spring, summer and autumn, but what of winter with bare trees and no bird song? It is not only because of the season that I suspect the calendar date of ' Hallowe'en ' as referred to in the ballad, but more because the first thing that Janet did on her visit to the wood, was to " pu' a rose . . . or twae " as she stood beside the well, where a riderless horse cropped the woodland grass. Naturally she expected the rider to return, which is why she waited, but she did not expect so gloriously handsome a youth to confront her, still less that he would chide her for having plucked a few wild roses. He explained his position as guardian of the woods on behalf of the Faerie Folk. Entirely overcome by his charm, it was not without intent that she asked if he had been Christened, and received not only an affirmation, but the history of his strange state, and the further confidence that he desired to return to a wholly human condition. In spite of the sombre local warnings, it was obvious that Janet needed no pressing to offer her help.

Tamlane's requests were then such as might well

have daunted a less courageous girl. He explained that every seven years on Midsummer Night the faeries had to pay tiend to Hell, and that he suspected that he had been chosen as victim that very night.

More anxious than ever to serve this fascinating faerie knight, Janet undertook to do whatever was necessary to save him from this awful fate and win for him release from the faerie existence.

"Tonight," Tamlane explained, "the Faerie Folk ride and I will be with them. You would need to be at Miles Cross at midnight."

"How will I know you among many others?"

"The first rider will be on a black steed. Say nothing, do nothing, let him go. The second will be on a brown horse. Say nothing, do nothing, let him go. I will be on the third, a white horse, with a gold circlet on my head, riding nearest the town and with my right hand gloved, my left hand bare, because I am a Christian knight. You must seize the reins of my horse and pull me from the saddle and hold on to me, Janet. If you love me do not release your grip no matter what betide."

So later that night Janet slipped out from the kindly tower, down to the strath, crossed the ford and hid at Miles Cross, until at midnight she heard an eerie rushing sound and the shrill notes of silver trumpets. Nearer and nearer they came, and her courage would have deserted her had she not thought of gallant Tamlane. The first knight came by on a black horse, and Janet said nothing, did nothing and let him pass. The second came on a brown horse, and Janet said nothing, did nothing, and let him pass. Then came Tamlane on a horse as white as moonlight, a gold circlet on his head, his right hand gloved, his left bare, and Janet sprang out and seized the reins and pulled him from the saddle. The Queen of Elfland appeared crying in anger. "You cannot have Tamlane, he is the finest of all my knights," and she turned him into an adder. Horrified and against her natural instinct, Janet held on. In a moment it was a giant newt she clasped, then a snapping fox, then an eel that almost escaped from her arms; a dove that almost escaped from her hands; a swan that beat its wings against her head; a burning stick that made her cry out as it blistered her hands; and still she clung, to find at last that her arms held a 'mother-naked man', her Tamlane whom she wrapped in her cloak and knew to be safe at last. But the Queen of Elfland was further angered.

"She has gotten a stately groom," she conceded, but told her erstwhile knight that if she had suspected that human love would attract him to such effect she would have "taen his heart o' flesh and gien him a heart o' stane."

The roofed and well preserved Tower of Oakwood, built on the site of the abode of Sir Michael Scott the Wizard by Robert Scott in 1602, still stands looking with peering windows towards the woods of Carterhaugh, where, on a still summer's evening, the beautiful trees still have an atmosphere of enchantment.

Thomas the Rhymer

Thomas the Rhymer, or Rimour, or, as given by Hector Boece, Thomas Liermont of Ercildoune, signed a charter in connection with Melrose Convent in 1189 and legend has it that he 'disappeared' in 1307. Ercildoune, now known as Earlston in Berwickshire, was once an important place where Thomas owned nine and a half acres.

With so small a farm, Thomas had time to indulge his talents for playing the clarsach and singing, which he often did for his own amusement, going into the woods to a favourite spot at Hunter's Bank under a thorn tree known as the Eildon Tree (eild -ron: uncanny, weird). Such hawthorns are frequently equated with magic in the folklore of Ireland and Scotland, and are probably remains of tree worship. The Eildon Tree was blown down in a gale in 1804 and though everything possible was done to replant and revive it, even to pouring wine on its roots, it did not survive, but on the east side of the Eildon hills near the Bogle Burn on the A6091 beside the road is a stone bearing the information that:

> *'This stone marks the site of the Eildon Tree where legend says Thomas the Rhymer met the Queen of Fairies and here he was inspired to utter the first notes of the Scottish Muse.'*

A man who remembers the tree says it was " a big tree with a trunk as thick as a man's waist, its branches a perfect circle, and roun' the tap i' the Spring a solid sheet o' white flourishing, scentin' the hale toun end, and its haws! There were na the like o' them in a' Scotland."

Reclining one summer's day in the shade of this tree, Thomas was surprised to hear the sound of small bells which, by their tone could only be of silver, and he saw, coming out of the wood, a dappled steed from whose reins the fifty-nine silver bells were suspended. The horse bore the most lovely lady Thomas had ever seen. She had long flaxen hair and a face so kindly that Thomas concluded she was Holy Mary, the Queen of Heaven, and knelt in reverence. But the lady denied such honour, assuring him that she was only the Queen of Elfland, or the 'middle-erth'. Her velvet cloak covered a green silk dress, which is the colour connected with the faerie faith, a circle of life which revolves eternally to Spring and its element of green. She wished him to sing and play for her, and offered payment of a kiss, but warned him that if he accepted her lips he would be hers and must serve her for seven years. Enchanted by her beauty, Thomas thought this would be a small price to pay, and what more could he desire than to be with her always? Under the spell of this magic embrace he mounted the horse behind her, and to the sound of the silver bells they departed at such a swift gallop that the wind could not outpace them. They came to a desert where was ' no living thing ' and there they dismounted, and Thomas lay his head in her lap. She showed him three roads, one was the narrow road of Righteousness, thick with thorns and briers, which the lady cynically referred to as one after which there were ' few enquiries '. The second road was wide among flowered fields and this was the path to Wickedness, which she admitted was called by some the road to Heaven; and the third, leading over ' the ferny hill ' was the road to Elfland which they would take. But before they remounted she had a warning to give him, namely that in her domain whatever he might see or hear or be asked, he was not to utter one word. If he contravened this order, he could never return to Ercildoune. This was a setback to one of such a temperament as Thomas, but under the magic of her personality he accepted the challenge, and they rode on to pass through blood and flood of roaring waters. It was over water that King Arthur went to the Isle of Avalon to taste the apples of eternal youth (which is why we dook for apples on Hallowe'en when spirits are abroad). Also immersion was the Druid rite for initiates, and tradition says that faeries or the spirits of the death cannot pass over water, and indeed the Druid rite connects with Christian baptism.

After such experiences, they came to an orchard where the Queen plucked an apple to give to Thomas " for wages," and said that the eating of it would give him " a tongue that could not lie." Thomas was very taken aback, as at home he was given to exaggerating in story-telling. Moreover, he wanted to know, how could he sell his cattle at a good price without exaggerating their value and hiding their faults? What of the lassies whose compliments must always be beyond their deserts? And how should he address persons of high degree who expected deviation from the truth in regard to their worth? But the faerie queen would have none of his excuses, and they so journeyed on to her realm.

For seven happy years Thomas kept silence till the time came for his reluctant return to Ercildoune, and after the return ride through the same diversities, he found himself back at Huntly Bank under the Eildon Tree. Here he beseeched that he might some time be allowed to return to Elfland and was told that when that should be granted the Queen would send messengers for him. With this he had to be content. He soon found that his truthfulness was taking an unexpected form, for he was able to tell the truth about the future, in fact he had Second Sight; indeed the date of his foretellings and their ultimate conclusions give room for reasonable credulity. Among his many predictions were the Battle of Bannockburn in 1314 and the Battle of Halidon Hill in 1333.

He also foresaw the decline of his own family:

> *The hare will kittle on my heartstane*
> *And there'll never be a Laird Learmont again.*

As Thomas became famous he also became wealthy, and it was his habit to entertain lavishly. On the occasion of one such feast, an attendant rushed in on the banquet to announce that a hart and hind were walking up the village street. Thomas recognised them as the messengers which the Queen had promised as a sign for his return to her ' middle erth '. So Thomas left his guests and joining the two deer he walked slowly in the moonlight into the silence of the woods from which he never returned. The belief that he will return again has reached as far afield as Inverness, where legend says:

> *When come the hosts of Tom na Hurich*
> *Who will arise but Thomas?*

45

Some hundred years ago a horse couper near Earlston believed that he had met and conversed with True Thomas. If there seems to be an Arthurian thread to the story, there is an obvious overlay of Christianity too, in reference to the three roads and the eating of the apple.

It is good to know that Thomas the Rhymer is not forgotten, for at the time of the Melrose Festival in the third week of June each year, the Faerie Queen rides on a white horse with Thomas mounted behind her, and they not only ride to the site of the Eildon Tree, but go to Gattonside to the ancient orchard of the monks where the followers partake of fruit proffered by men in monks' costume, as Thomas in his day ate of the fruit of Elfland and thereby gained his gift of prophecy.

On the outside of the eastern wall of the Church of Scotland in Earlston, on a stone removed from an earlier ecclesiastical building and now set under glass for preservation, are the words:

AULD RYMR
RACE
LYES IN THIS
PLACE.

Does that include Thomas? It is at least strange that his death was never reported.

The Worme of Linton

All over Scotland there are small hills and knolls
with serpentine indentations as if a great snake had
lain coiled round the sides. These date from as early
as Druidical times and, more often than not, the
sites are used for later churches, as is the case at
Linton in Roxburghshire, where the serpent or
dragon (the words are sometimes interchangeable)
was known as the 'laidely' Worme, and as the hero
of the event was a Norman, it would seem reasonable to assume that the word comes from the French
'laid' — ugly.

The creature lived in its hole at a place known
locally as Wormiston, likely on Linton Hill. It ate
animals to the extent of devouring whole flocks, and
suffered from acute bad breath:

> *No blade of grass or corn could grow*
> *So venomous was her breath*

So great a devastation had the Worme wrought that
even the people of Jedburgh, ten miles distant,
could not sleep easy in their beds.

Medieval arms were no protection, for arrows

bounced off its slimy skin and no one could get close enough, because of its breath, to cast a spear or drive a sword, and it is small wonder that the persistent deathroll of heroes who had attacked it, restricted further efforts towards its annihilation. It came to the point where the people gave up all hope of ever being rid of the monster.

Then, in the 13th century, John de Somerville of Lariston offered to attack it. Some say that he did so from a vehicle on wheels, which seems unlikely, for who or what could be persuaded to push or draw the vehicle into such danger? But the legend is insistent that the knight had a special spear made of unusual length, and its shaft sheathed with iron to withstand the heat of the creature's breath. Onto this spear he tied a sod of peat that had been dipped in pitch, which was to be lit when he was ready to try and drive it down the Worme's throat.

The whole countryside turned out to see the contest and admiration and joy was great when John charged at the monster and thrust the peat with its adhesive burning pitch down the creature's throat, and it writhed in the agony of death. The hero was knighted by King William the Lion (about 1211) and given the lands of the parish, as the old ballad says:

> *The wode laird of Lariston*
> *Slew the Worme of Worme's Glen*
> *And wan all Linton parochine.*

On the side of the mound which lies below to the east of the Church of Linton is a cavity looking like a bomb crater in which the creature was said to have lain at times.

Sir John is buried in the chancel of this little church that sits jauntily on top of the conical hill where the ancient tombstones stick out like pins in a pincushion. His family crest shows him killing the dragon and a tympanum over the door shows a very early stone carving of the event, in which the unusual length of spear is very evident. In 1954 an expert gave it as his opinion that it depicts not a dragon or serpent but two bears.

The little church at Linton shows records from the early thirteenth century, and among them is noted one Ralph de Somerville, an acolyte who, for some reason not stated, obtained a dispensation in 1255. Ecclesiastical buildings on this site were several times demolished, being so near the English Border, and Linton Tower of the Somervilles was destroyed by Henry VIII's troops.

There are many stories with less circumstantial evidence than this one, and in these days of discovery of live prehistoric fish and of monsters in Loch Ness and Loch Morar, there is little difficulty in giving some credence to The Laidely Worme of Linton.

The Gaberlunzie Man

The farm of Cairnkebbie on the estate of Foulden
was merry for it was celebrating the Harvest Kirn.
On the field the last sheaf was the target, each man
having a throw at it with his sickle, till one finally
brought it down to present to his favourite lass, who
dressed it with ribbons and, calling it The Maiden,
placed it in a prominent place in the barn. Here it
would remain until the New Year when it would
be fed to the oldest horse on the farm. The tenant,
William Hume, had supplied plenty of food and
ale for the dancing and ploys that would take place
in the Barn, but was at the same time looking
askance at one of his men, Bill Kerr, who was
obviously wooing the farmer's lovely young daughter
Lily. Her parents objected because they had ambi-
tions for the daughter beyond a farm labourer with
a light purse.

Everyone attending the Kirn was dressed in their
best. Bill had added a rosebud to every buttonhole
of his waistcoat, and Lily had pulled the folds of
her kirtle through its pocketholes in order to be
free to join in the long dances. Tam Luter, the

blind piper, had kept feet busy for an hour before a Gaberlunzie arrived, claiming the right of every such licensed beggar to join a festival feast. His dress was ragged and his wallets were apparently filled with the usual needs of bread and meal and spindles and whorles for sale to spinners, and he had his pipes under his oxter. Lily herself divested him of his bags and set them on a window sill while she provided him with his mug of ale. Having quaffed it, he decided to join in the fun and there was no room for inhibition in his method. He danced like a crazy gnat, leaping high in the air, throwing up his hat with its pheasant's feather, kissing the lassies, roaring with laughter and shouting " Hooch! Hooch! " with such blast as nearly rocked the old barn. Then he grabbed his pipes and seemed to intoxicate the dancers with excitement, dirling out tune after tune. Yet he noticed that his host's daughter was looking wistful, and he later took the opportunity to enquire the reason. Lily confessed that she and Bill were trysted but that her father was against the match because her man was poor. When the company was on the point of collapse from his wild cantrips, the Gaberlunzie started singing ranting songs and telling jokes that continued the merriment, and it was at this point that horses drew up outside the barn and a King's Messenger appeared with seven armed knights at his back.

" Silence! " he roared, " a beggar has this day stolen the Royal silver Mace. Here are witnesses at my back, and there is the man! " he cried, pointing at the beggar. " He did snatch the mace from the mace bearer's hands in the streets of Duns and made off with it."

" And if he ran as weel as he can dance," interrupted Williams, " the King's greyhounds wouldna get his heels."

The Gaberlunzie appealed to his new friends for protection, and all, including the farmer, having had their share of good ale and amusement, shouted that they would not give him up.

" He has partaken of my hospitality," said William Hume with dignity, " he is my guest and the merriest we ever had, and he had the right to the feast for his badge bears the Royal arms."

" Aye," shouted the guest, " I am Wat Wilson, the King of beggars."

" Search his wallets," commanded the Messenger, and, to the amazement of all, Wat Wilson said: " Give me my pokes." From one of them he produced the silver mace! Swinging it round his head, he shouted: " Come on now, ye hounds of royalty."

The crowd, excited and somewhat over-merry bellowed approval.

"We'll defend ye while there's a flail in the barn of Cairnkebbie," yelled the farmer, and every man reached for a flail or a keval (cudgel). The King's men unsheathed their swords but seemed loath to assault an unarmed crowd. During the ensuing stramash, Wat managed to manoeuvre the guests out of the barn and, with a quick movement, slammed the great door against the knights and shot the big bolts incarcerating the King's men. He shouted through the keyhole, "You may tell your King that I am the King of the Gaberlunzie men and have loyal subjects to defend me. But I am a gracious sovereign and when I pass through Duns the morn, I'll tell him that ye did no sae badly." With the mace under one arm and the pipes under the other, he strutted round the building to a stirring march. The farmer and some of the guests retired to the farm house to discuss the situation, and it was some time before they realised that the sound of a departing horse had meant that their merry friend was away with the mace and on one of the knights' horses.

Somewhat sobered, William Hume began to realise his position. He had sheltered and defended a thief against the King's men and helped him to retain part of the Royal regalia. It could go very hard indeed with him. He spent a sleepless night that was not altogether due to good fare, and his worst fears were realised next morning when the King's Messenger again arrived with a document. It accused him of assisting in the theft of royal property, of abusing and confining the King's knights and stealing a choice horse. He was therefore to attend the Court at Duns that day. It was signed James R. In his distress William appealed to the Officer to advise him how to better this tragic situation, and the advice was given to bring his daughter to the Court as the King liked to see a bonny face.

So the sad cavalcade of William Hume and his wife, his daughter and Bill Kerr, who refused to be left, made for Duns town and were there directed to the small castle that was used as a garrison for troops. In the great room to which they were conducted sat His Grace James V King of Scots, sumptuously apparelled, surrounded by his knights.

" William Hume of Cairnkebbie stand forth! " roared a voice. Trembling, William stood before his Sovereign while the Deemster read out the accusation.

" Is this true? " demanded the King.

William could not deny a word of it.

" You realise what the punishment could be for such a crime? "

" No less than my head, I doubt."

" Why did you defend this beggar? "

William launched into a description of the joy, the blitheness, the gaiety, the dancing, the merry piping; " a very king in all such things," he averred. His tale was met with a burst of laughter from James that was echoed by his knights.

" Have I won the wager? " the King asked them. " I challenged you that I as a beggar would so gain the approval of my subjects that they would loyally defend me against you."

" Yes, Your Grace has indeed won," and some of them were rubbing those parts of their bodies that had come into contact with flail and keval.

" Very well," said James. William Hume was in such terror waiting for the announcement of his punishment that he did not realise the import of the Royal joke and could not stop his knees shaking when the King added,

" I will now put on my cap to pronounce your fate." When William dared to look up it was to see the Royal head bedecked with the feathered hat of the Gaberlunzie, and in his hand the silver mace.

" Now, William Hume, I will be merciful on two conditions. One, that you permit the marriage of your daughter to Bill Kerr, to whom I am giving 200 merks as a marriage portion. Secondly, that you do not divulge who your guest was at the Kirn, and, for your defence of myself, I give to you the free grant of the lands of Cairnkebbie."

When the Barn again resounded to merriment, it was at the wedding of Lily and Bill, and the guests had only one lament, and that was that Wat Wilson the Gaberlunzie man was not with them.

The Bannock of Tollishill

If you turn left at Carfae Mill on the A68 south-
wards from Edinburgh, a winding road leads
upwards to the farm of Tollishill which, today,
trim and stark, overlooks the treeless hills, with only
sheep flocks to break the monotony of tone and
colour. Around 1647 the tenant was Thomas Hardie,
who, at the age of thirty, married a comely young
lass, Maggie Lyestone, who helped at the Inn at
Westruther. There he was a frequent visitor, walking the nine miles through the hills and back.

Not long after their marriage, the Lammermuir
hills suffered two successive winters of very heavy
snow and Thomas lost so many of his flock that he
faced ruin and at the Martinmas term could not
find money for the rent. The landlord, the Earl of
Lauderdale, was a hard man and the situation could
mean eviction. Faced with such tragedy, Maggie,
in spite of the heavy snow, set off to walk the eight
and a half miles to Thirlestane Castle, the great red
sandstone building with its two circular towers, that
was built on the site of the old fort, and which had
not yet the refinements added by later lairds.

Gaining admittance was not easy, but the Earl liked a bonny face and listened to the tale of the missing rent and promise of payment next year.

"You keep threeping about the long lying snow as an excuse for not paying rent," he bellowed. "It's myself that's like to be ruined. But I'll make a bargain with you," he added with a cruel smile. "With such late snow, you bring me a snowball in June and I'll forgo the rent." He roared with laughter. Maggie, battling her way home, was met by an anxious husband, who had resented asking favour of the Earl and was even more incensed at Lauderdale's cynical joke. But dauntless Maggie went secretly into the hills to a cleuch so narrow that it never saw the sun and there, in a small cave, she gathered snow into a hard pressed ball and blocked the entry with stones and wet moss.

On the first day of June Thomas was in despair and saw no reason for accompanying his wife with a large basket into the hills. Apprehensively Maggie pulled away the stones and there, gleaming white, was the snow, safely preserved in her primitive refrigerator. In great haste she set off again for Thirlestane where the dripping basket gained her quick entry. When the Earl was handed the snow-ball he was vastly amused and kept his promise of relief from the rent.

During the next few years good weather prevailed

and the Hardies became very prosperous. But if it was good fortune for them it was not so for Lauderdale. In 1647 Charles the First was dead. Cromwell was successful with his Model Army, and Lauderdale, supporting the Stewarts, was arrested and sent to the Tower of London. Most of the Earl's tenants were only too pleased of the excuse not to pay rent to an absent landlord, but the Hardies, remembering the Earl's generosity, put by the rent money year after year and, during the nine years of the Earl's imprisonment, it amounted to a considerable sum. It occurred to Maggie that if His Lordship had the money, it might serve to bribe his keepers and let him escape to France.

" Aye," agreed Thomas glumly, " but he cannae get it."

" We could take it to him," said Maggie.

" Are ye daft? Tak' it tae London! Walk all that way and be robbed afore we're twa miles ayont the Border! Moreover the road is no place for a bonny lass."

" I can dress as a laddie and I'll show you how we'll tak' the siller." Maggie made a bannock of exceptional thickness with pease and barley meal and secreted the money in the dough.

" Wha would think of stealing a bannock? " she asked.

They had won as far as Stevenage when they

accidentally met General Monk. 'Kind Geordie', as he was known, was not convinced with the disguise, and therefore conversed with them. Appreciative of the loyalty to a landlord, he promised to assist the release of the Earl of Lauderdale.

The couple had been three weeks on the road when they reached the Tower. Maggie, changed into normal attire and having blithely sung songs to the guards, asked the favour of being permitted to sing outside the window of the Earl's apartment. The song she sang was *Lauder's Haughs*, a tune which brought the prisoner to the window overwhelmed with nostalgia for the land he never expected to see again. Surprised at recognising his tenant, he asked that she might be brought to him.

" Well," he greeted her, " What have ye brought me this time? Another snowball? "

" No, My Lord, a bannock." When she handed it to him, he looked at it askance.

" Generous for size," he admitted, " but I doubt it must be somewhat stale."

" Aye, but pree it, my lord."

He broke it across his knee, revealing some of the coins.

" Nine years' rent. It's your ain siller," she said. Gratefully he kissed her hand.

" Ilka bannock has its maik (match) but (except) the Bannock of Tollishill," he said.

After their return home the Hardies learnt that General Monk had kept his promise and that the released prisoner had used the rent money to flee to France. Charles II had been crowned at Scone, and when it became safe for the Earl of Lauderdale to return, he was rewarded for his loyalty to his sovereign with high position. But that did not prevent him visiting the Hardies, accompanied with an extensive retinue, to thank them again for their loyalty to him in his absence. He called Maggie to him and placed round her waist a silver girdle of cunning workmanship which you may see today in the Museum of Antiquities in York Place in Edinburgh.

The Girl or the Gallows

Lacking the present day field sports, the hunt and the raid were a necessity in the Borders and Auld Wat Scott of Harden had, before his death in 1629, been a good tutor to his sons in this respect. So his eldest, William (later knighted by James VI), anticipated great enjoyment when planning a raid on Sir Gideon Murray of Elibank's famous herd. It would be natural that he should make use of his tower at Oakwood by the Ettrick to reach Elibank, rather than travel from the more distant house of Harden near Hawick, though he would finally drive the booty to Harden where a convenient deep gully offered a safe corral.

A good night's work it turned out to be, with Murray's cattle finally driven and herded near enough to the Yarrow ford for the reivers to relax and gather fuel for a supper of beef stewed in the skin. The sudden baying of a hound gave a warning but too late. With yells of " Elibank! Elibank! " Sir Gideon and his men were immediately laying about them in a manner that made the Scott retreat an urgent necessity. But Willie and his old hench-

man Simon were unwilling to turn their backs, and after a strenuous fight were taken prisoner. The Harden Scotts had a score against the Murrays since 1592 when a Murray and another member of the Scott clan had been given royal authority to destroy Harden as a punishment for Walter Scott having taken part in the Falkland plot against the King. With continual reprisals since then, it was unlikely that on this occasion William Scott would do other than hang at the end of a looped rope.

The castle of Elibank stands on the hill above the Tweed and from its sturdy ruins can be judged the position of the dungeon, the great hall, and the higher domestic apartments, as well as the surrounding buildings for retainers.

So it was with glee that Sir Gideon appraised his wife of his capture and the next day's hanging event, but she cut his jubilations short with the reminder that not only had they three unmarried daughters, but that one of them was far from comely and unlikely to attract a suitor, having the nickname locally of ' Muckle Mou'ed Meg '*, though her name was Agnes.

" Ye're no wiselike," she reproved him, " to hae a weel girt young man o' property in the hoose and talk o' a rope instead o' marriage."

* Big Mouthed Meg.

" But he'll no tak' oor Meg," objected her spouse.

" He will so, if you gie him the choice o' the girl or the gallows."

Sir Gideon had his doubts, but made the proposition, while Meg was told of her forthcoming possible chance of matrimony. Willie angrily scorned the suggestion in spite of his old retainer's pleas.

" Marry Muckle Mou'ed Meg? I'd as leif hang! "

Meantime Meg, having never expected such pleasant possibilities, did her best secretly to mak' siccar by disguising herself as a superior domestic, and stealthily taking extra food to the prisoners, engaging young Scott in conversation, offering to take a message to his mother, and assuring him that she would save him if she could. Though not impressed with her appearance, Willie acknowledged her gentle kindness and accepted her ministrations, while still letting the victor know in no uncertain language that he would rather be hanged than marry his daughter. So hanged he was to be and the next day he stood under the dule tree as adamant as ever with the rope round his neck.

Meg was present, well hidden at the back of the jubilating crowd gathered for such a rewarding event, and at the last moment when hands were ready to haul on the rope she whispered to her father to hold up the proceedings and ask the prisoner whether he would make the same refusal of marriage if the demand had been that he should wed the young domestic who had visited him in the dungeon.

Puzzled but intrigued, her father gave the message with the comment that ' the prisoner would be better saying his prayers than havering about a serving lass '.

" She wasnae bonnie," said Willie thoughtfully, " but she was a kindly, courageous wench, and a man could dae waur than tak' sic a wife."

At this statement, Meg shyly confronted him, admitting her deception. The condemned man, surprised and relieved, expressed his gratitude and consented to the marriage. So there was a wedding feast instead of a hanging, and the ugly daughter of Elibank married Sir William Scott of Harden. She is said to have been the best wife in the Borders bringing up a large family who were the progenitors of Sir Walter Scott the author.

The King's Hounds

The two daughters of Roslin, Elen and Clara, were at the Court of James VI, and as he made no secret of his admiration for Elen, the elder, no one was surprised that they were commanded to accompany the royal hunting party to the Elidon hills which abounded in game. Two witches (presumably the Carlins of Carlops) who were jealous of the two girls at nearby Roslin, turned them into white hounds over whom they retained complete control to do their bidding at certain hours.

White hounds are connected with Roslin as far back as the time that Robert the Bruce wagered the ownership of Pentland Moor against a Sinclair's head on the result of a chase with two white hounds.

Before the Elidon hunt, the two girls went missing, and the hounds presented themselves at the King's chamber to become his constant companions, joining in every hunt with unparalleled success; he named them Mooly and Scratch. But though the dogs brought down the quarry, no one ever saw the kill, until one day a shepherd called Crowdie, hearing the baying of the hounds as they

advanced, climbed up into the Elidon tree for safety while his dog Mumps fled for home. To the shepherd's horror, the dogs killed a girl but changed her into a doe before the huntsmen arrived. Moreover, while they were waiting for the hunt to catch up with them, Clara asked her sister,

"Will the King die tonight at the feast?" Elen replied:

> *The poison is distilled and the monk is won,*
> *And tonight I fear it will be done,*
> *But hush! hush! we are heard and seen*
> *Woe to the ears and woe to the een.*

Crowdie realised his responsibility to give warning and intended to inform Peri, a maid at Elidon Hall, that she might tell her master who would be at the feast. But the witches frustrated his intention by turning him into a swine. Accompanied by his puzzled dog the uncouth creature went to Elidon Hall for shelter and was kindly treated by Peri with the approval of her young lover Gale. Provisions for the approaching feast at the monastery of Melrose had to be found and the surrounding properties were supposed to supply their quota. The boar at Elidon Hall was considered an acceptable addition to the table. The knife was just going to be plunged into its throat (and the beast could offer no resistance being bound with Peri's red garters) when the two sisters passed at an hour when the witches had no power over them, and they compassionately returned Crowdie to his own shape. He immediately accused Peri of being a witch, of having turned him into a swine and then reversed the process, for proof, was he not tied with her red garters? She was therefore confined to prison, found guilty and due to be burnt. The kindly gaoler permitted Gale to spend her last night with her.

Meanwhile the feast at Melrose proceeded, the King being unaware of his fate, and with his two favourite hounds at his side he wished to propose a toast; no one doubted to whom it would be.

" My lords, I give you a toast to the fairest maid that ever Scotland bred — Elen of Roslin." But before cups could be raised, the Abbot suggested that the King's goblet should be filled with his favourite Malmsey wine of which they had a bottle in the cellar. Ralpho the servant was sent to fetch it, returned and filled the King's cup. But as the sovereign was raising it to his lips Mooly sprang at the goblet and spilled the wine. The shocked courtiers would have dispatched the dog immediately, but the King would not permit it.

" Let us see what she means," he said, then filled his cup with the ordinary wine which everyone else was drinking and put it to his lips. Mooly made no objection.

" We have not had the toast, Sire," reminded the Abbot. " Ralpho, fill my lord's cup with the good Malmsey wine."

When the cup was half-full, James challenged the servant to sample it. This he willingly did and within a few moments was writhing on the floor in death gasps.

" Treason! " was the shout, each accusing the other, and most suspecting the Earl of Angus. The King suppressed the riot and went to rest much troubled, taking his loyal canine friends into his bedchamber and setting a guard outside his door. He was wakened early next morning by a disturbance caused by two women insisting on an audience with him, accusing his hounds of having done away with two children at Newstead during the night.

" I can give you certain proof," said James, " that they never left my bedchamber." He called his guard to witness. But the embarrassed guard replied that though he knew that the hounds had not left the room, they had had to be let in at dawn. The old women demanded that the dogs be destroyed immediately. But remembering how Mooly had saved his life, the King insisted on further questioning. Douglas being suspicions, asked the women if they were willing to be baptised. One flew into such a rage that it was obvious she was a witch, and so was removed to be burnt at St. Michael's Cross. The other confessed and was permitted to leave. This eliminated their evil power over the sisters who resumed their own state, and the uncanny hounds disappeared. Elen and Clara were distressed for Peri whom they knew to be innocent, and for Gale in his sorrow, and obtained permission from the gaoler to visit them in prison. Having learnt something of the art of transmutation, they turned Peri into a moorhen and Gale into a moorcock, releasing them at St. Michael's Cross with the mysterious injunction contained in a ballad which bid them, " Hie awa' " but to " keep south of Skelfhill Pen." Pen may be short for Pentlands, a skelf is a thorn, and one of the witches of Carlops lived near a magic circle of ancient thorn trees on the north side of the Carlops Burn, so the warning was probably to keep away from that witch-haunted district. The verses furthermore added :

> *When five times fifty years have gone*
> *I'll seek thee again the heather among,*
> *And change they form if that age should prove*
> *An age that virtue and truth can love.*

On October 20, 1817, it was said that the Peri bird had been shot and eaten by friends of Wauchope in Edinburgh, which changed their natures to such an extent as to create a proverbial saying in the New Town of that day, to the effect that if anyone acted out of character it was said " He must have got a wing of Wauchope's moorhen."

The two sisters returned to Roslin, but their widowed mother was remarried to a pirate, so they retraced their steps to the magic Elidons and stepped into a Faerie Ring, which is why the court song says :

> *Lang may our King look and sair may he rue*
> *For the twin floers of Roslin*
> *His hand shall never pu'.*

Lochinvar

In writing his poem of *Lochinvar* Sir Walter Scott reversed the actions of the two men concerned. Why he should have done so is a puzzle. Had he a dislike of the House of Lauderdale? As a result of this inversion

> O Young Lochinvar
> Has come out of the West

are about the only two lines that are true in Scott's tale. Scott often bowed the truth to suit romanticism, but this is an extreme case. He digressed completely from his source of information which must have been the verses sung to James IV before Flodden by Lady Heron at Holyrood. This lady was the wife of the Captain of Norham Castle and as such she was rather resented at the Scottish Court.

The girl in this original story had the strange name of Katherine Janfarie, and it is permissible to consider it as a nickname connoting her characteristics of mockery and contention, for the Scots word ' jamf ' signifies ' to mock or trifle ' and ' farie ' is to create a stir, which she certainly did!

Katherine was bonny and well courted; among her admirers were both Lord Lauderdale and young Gordon of Lochinvar.

The former was secretive in his wooing and gained the young lady's favour, but they kept their trysting a secret from her parents. There must have been a reason for this unusual attitude, and it may well be that he was not free to marry her, but this did not mean that he was prepared to see her marry someone else, certainly not Lochinvar who was less successful in his courting, tho' doubtless the young jade led him on.

The old poem accuses Lochinvar of coming " oot frae the English Border," but from the position of his estate this charge could only allude to the family's original arrival with the Normans from the south, and the Lauder's were not in a position to throw such a taunt, having similar origins. Lochinvar, as Scott claims, ' came out of the West ' for his title is from the loch of that name in which there was an island where stood his castle. The island and its castle have been under water since 1968 when the level of the loch was raised, but you may see a cairn consisting of some of the castle's stones on the A702.

While Lauderdale was pursuing his romance, Lochinvar had obtained permission from Katherine's parents and kinsmen to arrange the wedding, but the bride was not to be informed until the actual day. From this somewhat unpardonable behaviour it may be assumed that the parents not only knew of the contesting secret romance, but also concluded that Lauderdale was not contemplating marriage, or why should they not have preferred the latter's suit as that from a noble of a powerful Scottish family?

When Katherine found out that she was to be married to Lochinvar that very day, her alarm and resentment was heightened by the absence of Lauderdale, who, she found out, was not to be one of the guests. Her protests were naturally emphatic, but her mother remained adamant to her daughter's raving.

" Ye have played around long enough. I ken ye, my daughter! Ye draw them tae your haund for a ploy and then laugh in your sleeve. All that's bye and ye'll marry young Lochinvar the day."

" So he's been playing ahint my back? What a husband to thole! " But the arrangements continued, and she dare not appeal to her father who was busy giving orders for the reception and the stabling of the horses of the approaching guests, for he would expect his daughter to obey her parents. So relations and friends arrived in numbers, all crowing with delight and ready to deck her in bridal array; but Katherine would have none of it.

" I wear my green silk," she said. Protests were many, for green was an unlucky colour for a bride, but Katherine was thrawn, and it was in her green dress that she mixed with the guests. Among them was a cousin who was perceptive enough to see through Katherine's dissembled gaiety, and she persuaded him to ride instantly with an urgent message to Lauderdale.

There followed an hour of apprehension for the bride, with Lochinvar triumphant in gay array, a whinger at his side and with a retinue of twenty-five of the clan Johnston at his back. Doubtless this piece of information was also conveyed to Lauderdale, for he arrived with twenty-five of his men from Lauderside.

Scott sets the scene at Netherby Hall on Cannonbielee, north of Longtown, which was a gey long ride either from Lochinvar or Lauder, and Katherine went frequently to her ' high window ' to await the arrival of her choice. When he came, each knew the need for dissembling, so she scoffed at his finery.

" Is it a Faerie Court you attend my lord? Or is it to fight that you come with a weapon at your side? I hope you will drink my health on this my wedding day? "

The understanding was mutual, and he made courteous reply,

> " I come na here tae fight
> I come na here to play
> I'll but lead a dance wi' the bonny bride
> And mount . . . and go my way."

This announcement must have been received with great relief by her parents and the bridegroom, who was justified in being anxious as to the behaviour of this braw example of the Scots nobility.

So with secret understanding as to his intent, the lovers pledged each other in wine, and then he took her

> " By the lily-white hand
> And by the grass-green sleeve,
> He's mounted her hie behind himsell,
> At her kinsmen spiered na leave."

> " Now take your bride Lord Lochinvar,
> Now take her if ye may "

challenged Lauderdale. To Katherine's delight there was a clash of swords and she noted that the craven Lochinvar and his followers "were not over willing."

> " Red and rosy was the blood
> Ran down the lily braes "

but the bride's enjoyment of the fray did not meet with her lord's approval.

> " My blessing on your heart sweet one
>   But nae to your wilful will,
>   For there's mony a gallant gentleman
>   Whae's blood ye've garred tae spill "

He added as a jibe to the retreating Lochinvar
that had Katherine gone in his company

> " On your wedding day
>   They'd gie ye frogs instead o' fish
>   And play ye foul foul play "

So disappears young Lochinvar on the best steed
in the Borders, by no means the character Sir Walter
Scott had conjured up of one

> " So faithful in love
>   And so dauntless in war "

The Master of Logan

The Master of Logan was a gay young spark. But, one day, in passing the kirkyard he stopped to have a word with John Telfer the grave digger, who had seen service with General Leslie. As in some of our older graveyards today, lack of room necessitated the removal of a previous tenant, and when John dislodged a skull and threw in on the grass, young Logan kicked it and was rebuked.

" That head," he was told, " was once adorned with gold and jewels, for the lady was a beauty from a village twelve miles distant, and though she was nae better than she should have been, ye should aye treat human remains with respect, young sir, for some of them dinnae rest easy, and return."

The Master of Logan was sceptical.

" What about her? " he sneered. " Do you think she might come and sup with me tonight? I could wish I might have such entertainment. You talk nonsense, John, there can be no life in rotting bone," and, putting the skull in one of his ancestor's tombstones, he rode gaily home, happy and hungry.

When he came to his table he was surprised and

annoyed to see it was set for two, and called his steward.

" How is this, Lockerbie? A table set for two? I dine alone."

" It is as was ordered, sire."

" I did not order it."

" No, sire, but between light and dark a messenger rode to the gate, rang the bell and announced that a lady would sup with the Master tonight. So I set for two."

" What manner of person with this messenger? "

" A pleasant man with a red face, but . . . "; there was a tone of uncertainty in Lockerbie's reply as he added, " Dick Sorbie swears it was a braw lass in a scarlet cloak wi' een like elf-candles, but I saw a man wi' a ruddy countenance."

Young Logan, for all his scepticism, was uneasy. He heard distant thunder around the hills of Tinwald, but he laughed at himself for thinking of things which had not entered his mind since his old nurse Martha had indulged in eerie bed-time stories.

Waiting for his meal, he sat on the old oak settle and looked at the portraits of his ancestors on the surrounding walls, and particularly at a picture depicting the Day of Judgement. He was suddenly afraid and, going to a cabinet of ebony, took out the old family Bible with its gold clasps. On the flypage, in his mother's writing, he read his name and the date of his birth and baptism. Old Telfer said that they sometimes want to return. Ridiculous! Peasant superstition! But he left the Book by his side when he rang the bell and bade Lockerbie bring old Rodan who had known and been trusted by his parents.

" I need your advice, Rodan."

" I can give you good advice, young sir, on such matters as agriculture or battles."

" No, Rodan, it is about neither."

" Then it's no' for me, sir, no' for me."

" It's about spirits."

" No' for me," repeated the old man, " for that you must seek the Minister, good Gabriel Burgess."

" Alright, I'll take your advice. Bid Sorbie saddle a quiet horse and lead it over the hill to Kirklogan, that he may bring the Minister to me in all haste."

Sorbie was puzzled. He had very frequently been sent errands to ladies on behalf of his master but never the Minister and he felt there was something chancy in the event, and sought to whistle to reassure himself as he jogged along with the extra horse. He whistled more loudly as he entered the shadowy Dead Man's Gill.

You may find this on the A75 near Byloch. A small road leads to West Denbie Farm, and the Gill was so named for the following reason.

Where the gully deepens as it enters the hills, there lived for a while the infamous persecutor of the Covenanters, Sir Robert Grierson of Lagg, and in the lower fields is a cairn which marks the site of the Court which condemned such Covenanters as were caught to be placed in barrels containing spikes to be rolled down the slopes of the Gill.

Such events having taken place only some twenty-five years previously, Sorbie feared the apparition of a victim, but he was agreeably surprised when a lady, cloaked and veiled, rode towards him on a palfrey.

" Is the Master of Logan at home? " she asked.

" Yes, my lady, but," he warned her, " he is expecting company for I saw the table set for two."

The lady lifted her veil revealing a face of exquisite beauty. She then continued her journey and Dick proceeded towards the Manse. He was even more surprised when he met the Minister afoot on his way to visit young Logan.

" How did you know to set out on this journey? " Sorbie asked.

" Premonition, lad." As they passed a small summer dwelling belonging to the family, the Minister glowered.

" A sinful spot," he said, " where men of his race have too often entertained more than they should, amongst their guests a wanton lass."

Meantime, things had been happening. The Master of Logan had heard a bustle of his servants at the door, and a lady approached his apartment with the rustle of silk in rich attire. Recognising her from a portrait he exclaimed, " Lady Anne Dalzell! "

" You must let me be a guest for an hour," she said, " for a storm is brewing and I must have shelter. Ah, I see the repast is ready."

Seated at the table she became talkative.

" I am now mistress of my own actions with no guardian to control me so I go where I wish and do as I wish." This statement was followed by the unbinding of her lovely hair and the Master wished he had not sent for the Minister.

Meantime the servants were gossiping.

" He named her the widow Lady Anne."

" Aye," said an old dame, " she passed away in 1656."

" Wheesht, that's no' chancy."

" Maybe no', but I'm telling ye that her faither, David Armstrong the Advocate, saw her marrit on the guid Sir Robert Dalzell of Ae. She haunts Dead Man's Gill."

The arrival of the Minister stopped their surmises and, on being announced, he sat himself between the two at the table.

" Aha! " he exclaimed jovially, " we have thoughts of the altar, no doubt! " and the Master of Logan had reason to be amazed at the good man's behaviour as the night wore on, for he drank and ate with gusto; laughed, and talked, but not on sacred themes.

The lady noted with disappointment that her host was not drinking and did not join in the merry banter; it was the Minister who kept her entertained. Moreover, she was even less pleased when her host insisted on relating his conversation with the gravedigger.

"You are aye in more jeopardy from rosy lips than dead bones," laughed the Minister. The annoyed lady tried to distract him by singing, but it was the Minister who joined in the chorus and stamped his feet to the tune. Such behaviour annoyed Logan but pleased the lady who asked the divine,

"I believe that you boast that you can discomfort evil spirits, good sir?"

"Indeed," laughed Gabriel Burgess, "if such should come, I would soon show you how I deal with them." He helped himself to more wine.

The Lady Anne looked at him slyly. She hoped that she might avert his power if he could be persuaded to use his influence on some inanimate object.

"If you have such powers, show us what you can do. Pretend this chair is an evil spirit and let us see the manner of your work."

The Minister consented by taking down a sword from the wall with which he described a circle and drew his host within it.

" Inside this circle," he said, " naught unholy can pass." He then filled a goblet with water announcing it as " the emblem of the purity of God," and flung it suddenly in the face of the smiling lady.

Anne Dalzell's mirth changed to a scream, her lovely locks became like serpents, her flesh shrivelled, and her eyes were illuminated with an evil glow. As she dissolved into air, she shouted at her host. " But for this subtle Minister you would have dined with me tonight in Hell." The Laird of Logan was on his knees in prayer. In a flash of lightning no more was to be seen of the strange visitor, and in the silence that followed Gabriel Burgess put a cup of wine into the Master of Logan's shaking hand.